BY
HELEN BANNERMAN

AUTHOR OF
"THE STORY OF LITTLE BLACK SAMBO"

NEW YORK
Copyright, 1903, by
FREDERICK A. STOKES COMPANY
PUBLISHERS
Printed in the United States of America,

The Story of Little Black Quibba

Once upon a time there was a little black boy, and his name was Little Black Quibba.

And his Mother was called Black Flumbo. But she was very ill, and had to lie in bed.

The Doctor came to
see her every day,
   And gave her nice
medicine

And nasty medicine.

But she got worse and worse, till at last the Doctor said she must die, unless she could get twenty mangoes to eat every day.

This made poor Little Black Quibba very sad, for he did not know where to find even one mango. However, he took the biggest basket in the house, and set out to see what he could find.

He asked everybody
he met,

But nobody could tell him where to find any.

At last he met a great big Elephant.

"Oh, Mr. Elephant," said he, "do you know any place where mangoes grow?"

Now this bad Elephant knew quite well, but he wanted to keep them all to himself, so he answered: " No, no,

no. I don't; I don't.
There is none this
way."

So poor Little Black
Quibba turned round
and went sorrowfully
back.

And the Elephant
stood and watched him
out of sight.

And Little Black Quibba went along a very long weary road, but he could not find any mangoes.

At last he met a Snake, and he asked it. "Oh yes," said the Snake, " I'll show you where there are lots of mangoes."

But he thought to himself: " When I get this nice fat little boy into the jungle, I'll eat him up."

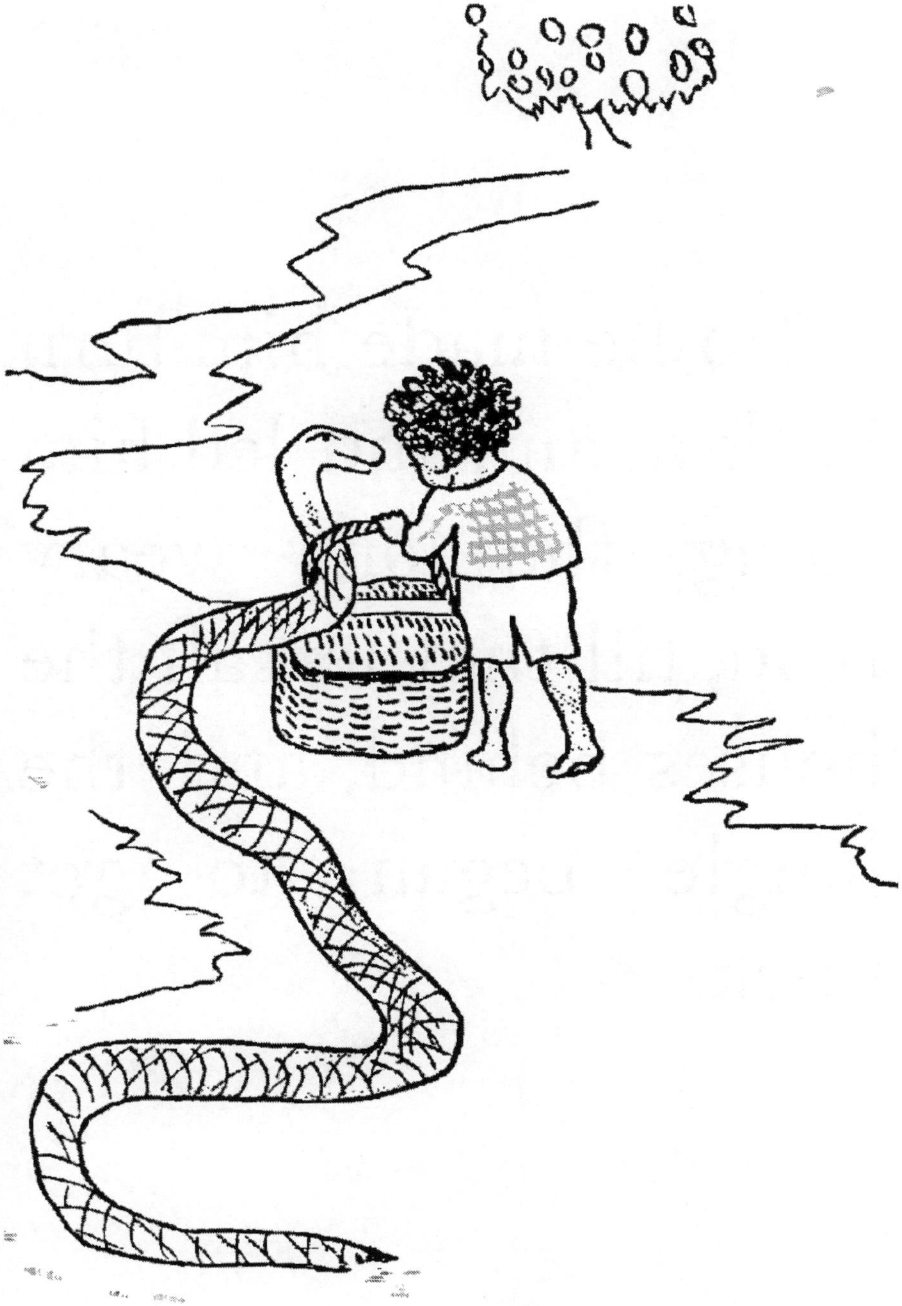

So he made him turn back again, and led him along the long weary road, till they left all the houses behind, and the jungle began to get thick.

Presently they met three frogs, and they croaked out: " Oh, Little Black Quibba, don't go with that Snake ; he eats people."

"Oh no, I don't," said the Snake; " I only eat grass."

But as soon as they had passed, the Snake made a dart back,

And when Little Black Quibba looked back he could not see the Frogs, and he began to suspect that the Snake had eaten them. This made him rather more watchful.

So they went on to-gether, and at last Little Black Quibba found himself in a splendid mango grove, with hun-dreds of trees, and thou-sands of ripe mangoes. Oh, how he jumped for joy.

When suddenly the Snake darted at him, hissing: " Ha, ha! Little Black Quibba, now I can eat you safely ! "

Little Black Quibba had just time to jump into the big basket, as the Snake dashed at him, and to pull the lid down.

Then the Snake tried to open the lid; but there was a loop of string inside, and Little Black Quibba held it firmly shut.

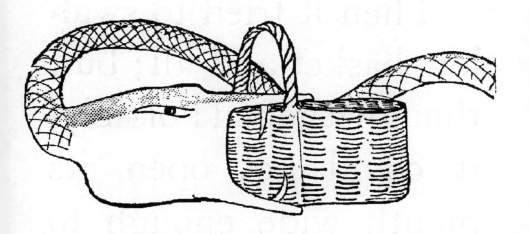

Then it tried to swallow basket and all; but, though it gaped horribly, it could not open its mouth wide enough to take the handle in.

So at last it climbed up on one of the mango trees, and hung the basket on a branch, and, curling itself round the stem, it pretended to go to sleep, hoping that soon Little Black Quibba would tire of the basket, and would try to get out.

Presently Little Black Quibba peeped out and was just going to try to get away, when up came the Elephant and said, "Oh! you are stealing my mangoes. I will throw you over the precipice."

"No, no," screamed the Snake; "I am going

to eat him up.   Take
him out of the basket
and give him to me."

"No, I won't," said
the Elephant; "you're
his friend," and seizing
the basket he swung it
over his head.

But the snake twined
round his leg and tried

to drag him back. The Elephant gave a great tug and fell over the precipice himself, and the basket, with Little Black Quibba in it, caught in a bush on the very edge, and Little Black Quibba scrambled out.

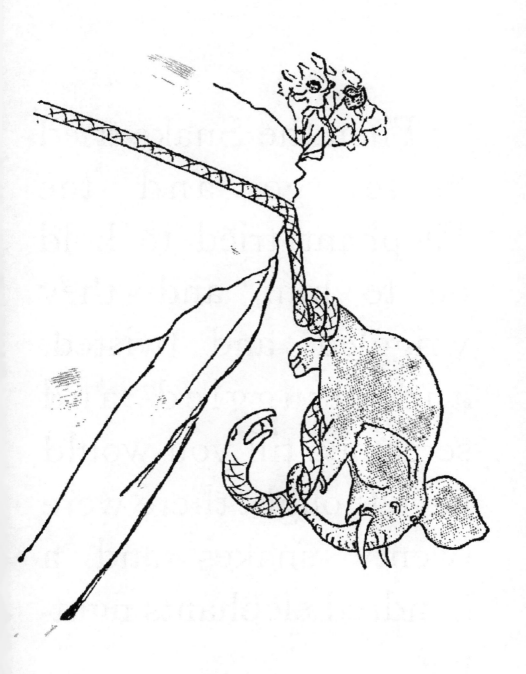

Then the Snake tried to let go, and the Elephant tried to hold on to him, and they wriggled and twisted, and struggled and screamed till you would have thought there were twenty snakes and a hundred elephants fighting.

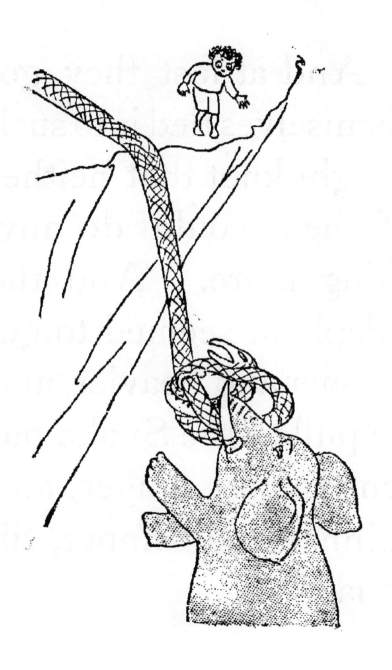

And at last they got themselves tied into such a tight knot that neither of them could do anything more. And the Elephant seemed to get heavier and heavier, and he pulled the Snake out longer and longer, and thinner and thinner, till at last

The snake broke with a *Snap!* into three pieces, and out jumped the little Frogs all alive and well, saying : " Didn't we tell you he ate people?"

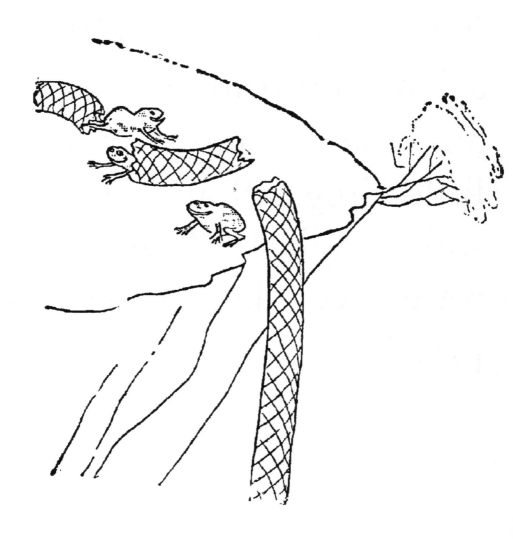

Meantime the Elephant was dashed to pieces on the rocks, far away below.

Then Little Black Quibba bravely scrambled over the Snake's tail and climbed up the tree, which he shook with all his might, and

Down came dozens of lovely ripe mangoes, all red and yellow, till the ground was perfectly covered with them.

D 165 813

How quickly Little Black Quibba filled his basket! Then putting it on his head he hurried home, smiling for joy.

As soon as he got home, he ran to his Mother, with a big mango in each hand. Even the sight of them made her feel better.

And before the bas-
ket was empty, she was
just as fat and just as
able to jump for joy as
Little Black Quibba
himself.